Return to the LAND of the MUSIC MACHINE™

Stories by Ane Weber
Illustrations by Mark Pendergrass

AGAPELAND® SERIES

Chariot Books

THIS I LOVE TO READ BOOK . . .

- has been carefully written to be fun and interesting for the young reader.

- repeats words over and over again to help the child read easily and to build the child's vocabulary.

- uses the lyrical rhythm and simple style that appeals to children.

- is told in the easy vocabulary of the validated word lists for grades one, two, and three from the *Ginn Word Book for Teachers: A Basic Lexicon.*

- is written to a mid-second grade reading level on the Fry Readability Test.

Chariot Books is an imprint of David C. Cook Publishing Co.
David C. Cook Publishing Co., Elgin, Illinois 60120

RETURN TO THE LAND OF THE MUSIC MACHINE
© 1984 by Agape Force

Text by Ane Weber
Illustrations by Mark Pendergrass
Printed in the United States of America

89 88 87 86 85 84   5 4 3 2 1

Library of Congress Cataloging in Publication Data
Weber, Ane.
    Return to the land of the music machine.
    Summary: Animals and things in nature demonstrate
ways to be honest, good, and fair.
    [1. Conduct of life—Fiction] I. Pendergrass,
Mark D., ill. II. Title.
PZ7.W3874Re 1984   [E]   83-24009
ISBN 0-89191-785-3 (pbk.)
ISBN 0-89191-836-1 (hc.)

Contents

=HERE SLOOPS, THERE SLOOPS=

Stevie liked to play pirate.

He rolled a piece of paper

into a circle.

He closed one of his eyes.

He looked into the long roll

of paper with his other eye.

He felt like a pirate.

The world looked like a bright

spot at the end of a tunnel.

He saw big, big flowers.

He saw tall, tall trees.

Suddenly, he saw something strange.
A big, pink, fuzzy thing!

"What is that?" Stevie cried.
He ran to the spot where the
thing was.
He walked around and around.
But whatever he had seen
was gone!

Something was here, Stevie thought.

I am going to catch it.

If it is a bird,

I'll catch it with seeds.

Stevie put some seeds in the grass.

Then he hid behind a tree and watched.

He watched and watched.

But nothing happened.

Maybe the thing is a big squirrel,
Stevie thought.

I will catch it with nuts.

He put some nuts in the grass.

Then he hid behind a tree and watched.

He watched and watched.

But nothing happened.

Maybe the thing is a big bear!

Stevie thought.

I will catch it with berries.

He put some berries in the grass.
Then he hid behind a bigger tree
and watched.
He wanted to be sure the bear
could not see him!

But this time something was different.
Stevie thought he was being watched!
Slowly Stevie turned around.
There stood a big, pink, fuzzy thing!

It was no taller than Stevie.

It was covered with long fur.

It stood on two legs and had two arms.

Its hands looked like soft mittens.

And it was smiling!

"Hi!" said the thing.

"I am a sloop."

Stevie was surprised to hear

the thing talk.

Suddenly, more sloops came
out of the woods!
There were big ones and little ones.
Fat ones and thin ones.
Red ones and yellow ones.
And they were all smiling!

"I see you have met the sloops,"
said a familiar voice.

Stevie turned toward the voice.
It was Mr. Conductor.
And Nancy was with him.
"We have been playing with the sloops,"
Nancy said. "We tried to find you."

Now the pink sloop spoke again.

"I told them I'd bring you back.

But you seemed to be afraid of me.

Yes, I am different.

But different things are often nice."

"Come on, Stevie," Nancy shouted. "You almost missed out on all the fun! The sloops play the best games."

So Stevie and Nancy

played with the sloops all that day.

They played Touch-the-Tree and

Catch-the-Moon and Save-the-Sloop.

They jumped and ran and climbed.

The sloops did play the best games

in all of Agapeland!

══THE HONEY TREE══

Everyone knew that Mr. Bee made
the best honey in all of Agapeland.
And everyone came to his honey
tree to get some honey.
So Mr. Bee worked very hard to
make his honey good to eat.

One day Mr. Bee thought,
Why should I give my honey away?
From now on I will ask for
something in return.

Just then there was a *tap, tap*

on Mr. Bee's door.

It was a little brown mouse.

"May I have some honey?" he asked.

"Yes, you may," answered Mr. Bee.
"But you must give me something
in return."

"All I have is this little gold bell,"
said the brown mouse.
Mr. Bee looked at the bell.
He shook it.
Ding-a-ling, ding-a-ling.
He liked the sound it made.

"That will do," said Mr. Bee.

He gave the brown mouse some honey.

Mr. Bee put the bell in his honey tree.

Just then there was *peck, peck*

at his door.

It was a beautiful bird.

"May I have some honey?" she asked.

"Yes, you may," said Mr. Bee.
"But you must give me something
in return."

"All I have are my beautiful
feathers," said the bird.
Mr. Bee looked at her feathers.
He liked all the bright colors.
Red and blue and green.

"A blue one will do," said Mr. Bee.

He gave the bird some honey.

Mr. Bee put the feather

in his honey tree.

Soon Mr. Bee's tree was filled

with many things.

Fruit and flowers,

rocks and sticks,

and much, much more.

Mr. Bee spent a lot of time

looking at his things.

He had little time to make honey.

He had little time to see his friends.

So they stopped coming

to his honey tree.

Soon Mr. Bee grew very sad.

"Buzzzzzzzzzzz.

Look what I've done," he said.

"I have taken things in return
for my honey. Now I have many
things—but no friends."

Mr. Bee had an idea.

He gave away all his things.

Once again his honey tree was empty.

Then he went back to making honey.

Mr. Bee saw the little brown mouse.
He saw the beautiful bird.
"Please come to my honey tree,"
he said. "I'd like to give you
some honey. I will not ask for
anything in return."

Soon Mr. Bee's friends came
back to his honey tree.
"Now I have many friends,"
he said. "But few things.
Now I am very happy."

═THE BLUE SLOOP═

A long time ago Blue Sloop

lived in Agapeland.

There were red sloops.

There were green sloops.

But no other blue sloops.

Yet Blue Sloop did not feel special.

He felt big and furry and plain.

Blue Sloop was not content.

One day Blue Sloop walked

in the forest.

He smelled the flowers.

Hmmmm! They smelled good.

He smelled his fur.

It smelled damp.

He wanted to smell as

good as the flowers.

He saw the beautiful colors
of the peacock.

Red and blue and yellow and green.

Blue Sloop looked in a pond

to see himself.

He saw a large, furry, blue figure.

He wanted to be as pretty

as a peacock.

Blue Sloop heard a little bird

singing in the trees.

"Tweet! Tweet! Tweet!"

Blue Sloop tried to sing.

"Hum! Hum! Hum!"

His voice was low and scratchy.

He wanted to sing like a bird.

Everywhere he looked
Blue Sloop saw something that
smelled better,
looked better,
and sounded better than he did.
Blue Sloop was not content.

Then Blue Sloop had an idea.
He ran into the woods.
He picked all the flowers
he could find.

He got all the peacock feathers
he could find.
He caught the little bird
and put it in a gold cage.

Blue Sloop went to work.
He made a tall, tall hat out of
the peacock feathers.
He made a long, long coat out of
the flowers.

He put a vine through the
golden cage.
Then he put on the tall, tall hat
and the long, long coat.
He put the cage around his neck.

Blue Sloop went back to the pond.
He looked in to see himself.
"Now I am the most beautiful
sloop in the land," he said.
"Now I will be content."

But when the other sloops
saw Blue Sloop, they laughed.
"You look so very, very funny,"
they said.

The birds didn't think
he was so funny.
They were angry.
"Why did you catch our friend

and put him around your neck?"

they asked.

They bit him with their beaks.

Just then some bees saw Blue Sloop.

They liked his flower coat.

They flew all over him.

buzz, buzzzzzz, buzzzzzzzzzzzzz.

Blue Sloop was afraid.

He ran and ran and ran.

But he could not run faster than the bees.

So he ran to the edge of the pond.

He untied the cage and let it fall to the ground.

He jumped into the water.

Splash!

The bees did not like the water.

Soon they flew away.

Blue Sloop climbed out.

He looked in the pond to see himself.

His tall, beautiful hat was wet.

His long, beautiful coat was wet.

Blue Sloop knew he looked
silly.

His face felt hot.

It turned pink.

Then rose.

Then red.

Blue Sloop was no longer blue!
Now he was red from the top of his
head to the bottom of each foot.

When the other sloops saw him,
they asked, "What happened?"
"I could not be content,"
Blue Sloop answered.
"I wanted to be special.
Now I'm red just like the other

red sloops.

But I have learned my lesson.

I will be content."

Blue Sloop even changed his
name to Be Content.
But he never turned blue again.
Try as you might, you will never
find a blue sloop in all
of Agapeland.

—THE TREE HOUSE—

Simon Sloop lived in a tree house.

His friends Fred and Ernie

lived in tree houses, too.

One day Fred and Ernie came

to Simon for help.

They both thought Simon

was very wise.

"Ernie is afraid of high places,"

said Fred.

"I am afraid to climb up

to my tree house," Ernie said.

"When I look down,
the ground is so, so far away.
Maybe I should move out of
my tree house."

Simon thought for a moment.
"You don't need to move," he said.
"But you do need to get over your
fear. Wait here. I have an idea."

Simon climbed up to his tree house.
Soon he came down with some rope
in his hand.

The three sloops walked
to Ernie's tree house.
Simon made the rope into a ladder.
Then he tied the ladder to a big,
strong branch high up on the tree.
"There," said Simon. "Just walk up
this ladder to your tree house.
But don't look down, Ernie."

Ernie started up the rope ladder.

Up, up, up he climbed.

When he was near the top,

he thought, *I made it!*

He looked down to thank Simon.

"Don't stop!" shouted Fred.

"Don't look down!" shouted Simon.

But it was too late.

Ernie had already seen the ground.

His red face turned white with fear.

He ran down the ladder

as fast as he could.

"It's no use," said Ernie.

"I should move out of my tree house."

"Don't worry," Simon answered.

"I have another idea."

Simon found a piece of wood.

He put a piece of grass on the wood.

"Just put this around your neck
and climb back up the ladder.
If you look down,
you will see the grass.
You will think you are near the
ground."

Ernie tied the piece of wood
around his neck.
Up, up, up the ladder he climbed.

But the grass tickled Ernie's nose.

"Ah . . . ah . . . AHCHOOOOO!"

The piece of wood came loose.

Ernie watched it fall to the ground.

His red face turned white
with fear.

He ran down the ladder
as fast as he could.

"It's no use," said Ernie.

"I should move out of my tree house."

But Simon did not give up.

He thought and thought and thought.

Finally he had another idea.

"Look up there, Ernie," said Simon.

"Your tree house is not far away
from the ground.

It is close to the sky!

And you love the big, blue sky."

Ernie took hold of the ladder.

"I do love the sky," he said.

"So there is no reason to be afraid."

Ernie took a deep breath.

He closed his eyes and

climbed up, up, up.

Once he reached his tree house,

he wanted to look down.

First he looked a little.

Then he looked a lot.

"Look at me," he shouted.

"Now I am not afraid.

Now I do not have to move.

I will live in my tree house

forever and ever and ever."

THE TUNE-UP

One day Stevie and Nancy heard
a strange noise.
Clang, clang, clang,
Mr. Conductor was working on
the Music Machine.

He turned some dials.
Creeeeek! Creeeeek!
He turned some knobs.
Creeeeek! Creeeeek!
"There," he said.
"That should do it.

Let's see if the Music Machine works."

"Nancy and I would like to ask
the Music Machine a question,"
Stevie said.

"What is the most important
thing in all Agapeland?"

"Maybe it's the flowers," said Nancy.
"No," said Stevie. "I think it's
the animals that talk."

"I know," said Nancy. "It's the
Music Machine itself."

Whir, whir, chuka, chuka,
bomp, bomp, psst.
The Music Machine began to bubble
and shake.
Then it began to play a beautiful
song. It was about love.

But before the song was over,

the Music Machine slowed down.

It slowed way, way, way down.

Whir . . . whir . . .

chuka . . . chuka . . .

bomp . . . bomp . . . psssssst!

"The Music Machine stopped,"

Nancy shouted. "What can we do?"

"I don't know," said Mr. Conductor.

"I already gave it a tune-up.

Maybe you children can make

the machine work."

"Us!" Stevie shouted. "How?"

"Maybe the Music Machine is cold,"
Nancy said.

She put a scarf around the Music

Machine. But nothing happened.

"The Music Machine has roots

like a tree," said Stevie.

"Maybe it needs water."

Stevie and Nancy found two

watering cans.

They filled them with water.

They poured the water around the

machine's big, thick roots.

But nothing happened.

"If only we knew how to fix it,"
Nancy cried. "We would do
anything to help."
"We love the Music Machine,"
Nancy and Stevie said together.

Just then they heard a wonderful
sound.

Whir, whir, chuka, chuka,

bomp, bomp, psst.

The Music Machine began to play.

It played the song about love.

"We did it!" shouted Stevie.

"We fixed the Music Machine!

And now it is answering our question.

Love is what makes Agapeland so

special!"

"That's it!" cried Nancy. "Don't you see? Everyone needs love, because God is love.
All the Music Machine needed was love!"